THE BEST PETS YET

All inquiries should be addressed to:
Barron's Educational Series, Inc.
250 Wireless Boulevard
Hauppauge, NY 11788

ISBN-13: 978-0-8120-4857-5
ISBN-10: 0-8120-4857-1

Library of Congress Catalog Card Number 91-39904

Library of Congress Cataloging-in-Publication Data

Foster, Kelli C.
　　The best pets yet/ by Foster & Erickson; illustrations by Kerri Gifford.
　　p. cm. (Get ready–get set–read!)
　　Summary: A girl looking at clouds of different shapes is reminded
of a variety of pets, all of which she would like to have.
ISBN 0-8120-4857-1
　　(1. Pets–Fiction.　2. Clouds–Fiction.　3. Stories in rhyme.)
I. Erickson, Gina Clegg.　II. Russell, Kerri Gifford, ill.　III. Title. IV. Series:
Erickson, Gina Clegg. Get ready–get set–read!
PZ8.3.F813Be 1992
(E)–dc20　　　　　　　　　　　　　　　　　　　　　91-39904
　　　　　　　　　　　　　　　　　　　　　　　　　　CIP
　　　　　　　　　　　　　　　　　　　　　　　　　　AC

PRINTED IN CHINA
20

GET READY...GET SET...READ!

THE BEST PETS YET

by
Foster & Erickson

Illustrations by
Kerri Gifford

BARRON'S

I never met a pe

that I didn't like yet.

Look up!
What is that pet?

Oh yes,
it is a very pretty pet.

This pet likes to get wet.

I like to get wet
with my green pet.

You can get
this pet with a net.

But I must be fast
to get the pet.

This one is a funny pet.

Up, up, up—
it likes to jet!

I take this pet
to see the vet.

Vets help pets.

I bet you would
like this pet.

I won't forget
how I got this new pet.

No, I never met a pet
that I didn't like yet.

The End

The ET Word Family

bet
forget
get
jet
met
net
pet
pets
vet
vets
wet
yet

Sight Words

my
new
one
won't
look
very
didn't
funny
green
never
would
pretty

Dear Parents and Educators:

Welcome to *Get Ready...Get Set...Read!*

We've created these books to introduce children to the magic of reading.

Each story in the series is built around one or two word families. For example, *A Mop for Pop* uses the OP word family. Letters and letter blends are added to OP to form words such as TOP, LOP, and STOP. As you can see, once children are able to read OP, it is a simple task for them to read the entire word family. In addition to word families, we have used a limited number of "sight words." These are words found to occur with high frequency in the books your child will soon be reading. Being able to identify sight words greatly increases reading skill.

You might find the steps outlined on the facing page useful in guiding your work with your beginning reader.

We had great fun creating these books, and great pleasure sharing them with our children. We hope *Get Ready...Get Set...Read!* helps make this first step in reading fun for you and your new reader.

Kelli C. Foster, PhD
Educational Psychologist

Gina Clegg Erickson, MA
Reading Specialist

Guidelines for Using *Get Ready...Get Set...Read!*

Step 1.   Read the story to your child.

Step 2.   Have your child read the Word Family list aloud several times.

Step 3.   Invent new words for the list. Print each new combination for your child to read. Remember, nonsense words can be used (*dat, kat, gat*).

Step 4.   Read the story *with* your child. He or she reads all of the Word Family words; you read the rest.

Step 5.   Have your child read the Sight Word list aloud several times.

Step 6.   Read the story *with* your child again. This time he or she reads the words from both lists; you read the rest.

Step 7.   Your child reads the entire book to you!

Titles in the

Series: